Saved by Grace

Saved by Grace

Blessed with Twins

Lorena Dove

Printed in the United States of America

First printing, 2017

ISBN-13: 978-0-9964744-2-9

Published by Royal Glen Studios, LLC.
www.RoyalGlenStudios.com

Dedication

To all who have a song in their heart.

Preface

In **Saved by Grace**, a widowed farmer is ready to take a new wife, but his twins Willie and Annabelle want to have a say in his choice. Grace Haggerty brings love, laughter and music back into their home, but can Will trust his heart to marry for love again?

Thank you for letting me know through your emails, Facebook comments and reviews that my "little stories" bring you joy, laughter, tears and a word of encouragement! It's an honor to have such wonderful readers.

Enjoy your trip back to a simpler time,

Lorena Dove

~Author of inspirational western romance fiction

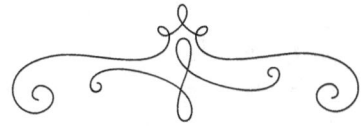

Chapter One

"Mama! Hurry!" Annabelle screamed over the sound of the wind as her mother, Anna Forrester, struggled against the wind to shut the door to the barn.

"I'm coming," she yelled back. "You and Willie get down!"

"Get in here!" Willie grabbed at his twin sister's dress. "Loretta says to get away from the steps!"

Annabelle followed Willie down into the storm cellar and huddled against Loretta's body in the dark. "You children listen to me now, and to your mother! Ain't no time to be sassing anyone when a tornado's coming!"

"Yes, Loretta," Willie said.

Annabelle just hugged her tighter and watched for her mother to appear at the top of the steps.

Anna Forrester took one last look around the yard, satisfied she had gotten all the animals safely into the barn. She stared in disbelief at the swirling dark cloud barreling across the fields toward her. Will had mentioned there might be afternoon thunderstorms today, and he promised to be back from town before the weather got bad. But the sky had turned yellow and then an odd shade of green before he returned. It was now an ugly grey-black. She saw the swirl of brown dirt, white laundry, a piece of a fence, tree limbs and other things she couldn't make out in the whirling, mauling mess.

"I'm coming!" she yelled, but no one heard her. She ran to the storm cellar, climbed down a few steps, and turned to reach for the door handle to close it over them in the dark.

The sound of Loretta's praying came to her ears, along the sobs and tears of Annabelle and Willie. She reached with all her strength and started to pull the door up from the ground. A gust of wind slammed the door back to the ground, pulling her forward and halfway out of the cellar.

"Mama!" The twins cried in unison.

"Oh Lord, help us in our time of need, Dear Jesus, watch over us...." Loretta's praying grew louder.

"I'm all right!" Anna yelled as hard rain started to pelt down on her. She found her footing, and felt a hand on her leg. She looked down into the somber eyes of her five-year-old boy. "Willie, get back!"

"No! I'll hold onto you!" he yelled up at her.

She didn't have time to argue. She must get the door shut before the tornado was directly on them. The wind tugged at her and she could feel Willie pulling back with all his might. She grabbed the door handle and pulled it up again. With a mighty heave, she pulled it down over their heads.

Willie fell to the floor still holding her leg as his mother came crashing into the cellar. All was dark and a bit quieter as Loretta continued praying.

"Mama!" Annabelle screamed. Anna stood to reach for her in the dark.

A crashing sound rolled through the cellar and suddenly the door ripped off its hinges and flew away into the dark sky. Anna's body rose through the door right behind it, with little Willie still hanging on as long as he could.

Loretta and Annabelle lunged forward to grab onto Willie as rain soaked them all.

"Mama! Mama!" he cried inconsolably, waving his empty hands in the air.

Chapter Two

Two years later...

"Time for breakfast," Loretta called from the kitchen.

"Come on, I smell bacon!" Annabelle said. At seven, she was up early to feed the chickens.

Willie began to replace his treasures into the wooden cigar box. He had finished feeding the goats and had climbed into the hayloft before Annabelle could finish. He picked up his marbles, a long piece of string, and some pennies and dumped them into the box. He held a small woman's comb in one hand and looked at it intently. The porcelain was cracked and chipped, but he traced his finger around the faded pink roses and down the green vine. He kissed it and put it into the box.

"I said, come on!" Annabelle's golden head popped up through the ladder opening.

Willie nodded and hid the box against the side of the barn behind a hay bale.

"I know what you keep up here!" she teased. Willie looked at her with surprise in his eyes. "Don't worry, I won't tell," she said.

Willie climbed down after Annabelle. The twins held hands to hold each other back from racing to the kitchen, ensuring neither one could be declared the winner. They squeezed through the doorway together and got to their seats at the same time.

"Aren't you children forgetting something?" Loretta admonished them.

They looked up in surprise, each with a hand in the air over the delicious smelling plate of bacon in the middle of the table.

"Oh, wash our hands!" Annabelle said, laughing.

Willie was already up and at the sink. They splashed their hands together under the water, the smell of bacon, muffins and eggs on the stove enticing them to finish as quickly as possible.

"Here now," Loretta said, handing them each a soft cotton dish towel. "Let's leave most of the dirt go in the sink and not on my clean towels!"

"Mine are clean!" Annabelle said and held up her hands. Willie did the same.

Loretta inspected them. "All right, Annabelle. Willie, yours will do, but next time use some soap."

Willie nodded and jumped back into his seat, helping himself to bacon and a muffin as Loretta spooned scrambled eggs from the pan onto their plates.

"Good morning, children! Good morning, Loretta!" a man's booming voice broke into the kitchen followed by the tall frame of Will Forrester.

"Good morning, Father!" Annabelle said.

"'Morning, Mr. Forrester," said Loretta.

Willie smiled up at his father.

Will bent down and kissed Annabelle on the cheek, walked around the table, and gave Loretta a passing hug. He came behind Willie and laid a hand on his shoulder.

"I said, 'Good morning, Willie'," Will said.

Willie looked down and then back up at his father. His chin moved in a small nod.

Will kept his son's gaze as he pulled out the chair next to him and sat down. "Just a little hello?"

Willie's eyebrows went up and he shrugged his shoulders. He put a piece of muffin in his mouth.

Will sighed. "Well then, maybe tomorrow. How's my prettiest ray of sunshine?" he said to Annabelle.

"I'm fine, Father. Willie's fine, too. We've already done our chores. Won't you take us to town with you today? Please, Father?"

"No, I won't," Will said slowly, enjoying the momentary drop in Annabelle's countenance. "But, I will let you stay up late after supper tonight. I'm inviting some very special guests."

"After supper? You mean—is it a party?" Annabelle asked hopefully.

"Not a party, really..." Will said. "Well, we're having some folks over for supper, and someone special is coming that I want you to get to know."

"You mean Mrs. Thompkins and her friends," Loretta sniffed from the sink. "I hope she likes children."

"Loretta! Of course she likes children." Will said, surprised. "Why, she's the headmistress at the school, isn't she?"

"Headmistress! School! Oh, Father, are we going to school?" Annabelle asked.

Willie slunk further into his chair.

"It's about time you children got off the farm. First grade for you both come September. Yes, Willie, you too," Will said, noticing the grimace on his son's face. "You can't spend all your days chasing frogs and bedeviling Loretta in the house. It's time you learned to read and write as well as Annabelle can."

"Mother taught us both," Annabelle said. "Willie can read, just like he can talk ... if he wants to."

"Well, it's time," Will said. "After we lost your mother, I admit I didn't want you two to be out of my sight most days. But it's been two years, and you need to be in school with other children. And I need ..." He stopped short.

Annabelle and Willie looked at him. Annabelle's fork was paused mid-air, and Willie's face had clouded over at the mention of their mother.

"Well, I need companionship, too," Will said. He shifted uncomfortably in his chair.

Annabelle got up and hugged her father. "But you have us," she said. "And Loretta."

Will patted her hand. He reached over to Willie and took his hand also. "We'll always have each other. And maybe soon, someone to look after us."

"Hhmmph!" Loretta snorted.

"Present company excepted!" Will said, laughing. "Loretta, I don't think I've ever had as fine a blueberry muffin as this one right here. Isn't that right, children?"

"Yes, they're delicious!" Annabelle said, skipping over to give Loretta a hug. "Aren't they, Willie?"

Willie stuffed half a muffin into his mouth, and smiled with crumbs covering his lips. Will, Annabelle and Loretta burst into laughter. His shoulders shaking, Willie silently chuckled along with them.

It's good to see them laughing, Will thought as his mind turned to them meeting Miss Harriet Thompkins that evening. *I hope, for their sakes, they'll accept her into our lives*

Chapter Three

race Haggerty waved good-bye to her last piano student of the day. The little girl turned and waved, clutching her music book in the other arm, as her mother led her down the sidewalk.

Grace let the curtain fall from the window and turned back to the darkening room. She sighed, went over to the table, and lit a lamp. She admired the dark blue and reds of the stained-glass lampshade casting its warm glow into the room.

It's so pretty, she thought, taking a seat on the parlor sofa and picking up her latest book to read. She slipped off her shoes and rubbed her toes, first one foot and then the other. Tomorrow night was the recital and she'd be done for the summer with her students. She had the summer to look forward to... but no real plans. As much as she needed time off from teaching, she dreaded the long, lonely days ahead.

Bzzz! Bzzz! Someone pushed the buzzer multiple times before she could get back to the door.

"Grace! Grace! I have good news!" said Patty Owens as she bustled in.

"Come in," Grace said, laughing as she shut the door behind her sister, who was already in the parlor.

Patty turned around to face her. "Come sit! You'll never believe what just happened." She sat down and patted the sofa next to her. "I was finishing my shopping, you know, just browsing around the store," Patty started. "Whoo! I have to catch my breath! I ran all the way here."

"Really, a married woman shouldn't be running down the street, should she? What will people think?"

"Positively shocking, I know! But I didn't care. I had to come tell you the news."

Grace shook her head. *If Patty's this excited, it can only mean trouble for me.*

"So as I said, oh, can I have a sip of your tea?" Patty interrupted herself to lift Grace's cup to her lips. "It's gone cold! Oh, never mind! As I was saying, I was in the store, my basket full of the cutest new hat and gloves, and I was just browsing around for a bit, when in walked – well, guess!"

"I can't possibly guess," Grace said, smiling at her sister. "Why don't you tell me?"

"No? Not even a try? Oh well, it was Mr. Ratlinburg! You know, the owner of Ridgewells?"

"Yes, I've heard of him."

"Can you imagine? He owns the finest shops in the county, and the biggest store in Philadelphia! Anyway, he was there with his daughter—I know her from the Ladies' Circle. We got to talking, and she invited Charles and I—and you!—to the Princeton Alumni dinner Saturday night! Can you imagine?"

"But Charles didn't go to Princeton," Grace began.

9

"No, but Cornelia invited us just the same! I think, to be honest, she was thinking of you."

"Why? What would she have to think of me about?"

"Well, I took the liberty, I hope you don't mind, but I just had to take the chance to tell her all about you."

Grace sighed. Patty was so bubbly she couldn't help herself, but Grace was mortified to know she was blabbing her personal business around town.

"Patty! I've asked you again and again, please don't talk about me to your friends! I'm not just a piece of furniture or a new hat, for goodness' sakes!"

"No, you're not. You're a flesh-and-blood, live human, and a lovely woman with no prospects—Oh! I didn't mean that," Patty said. "That didn't come out right at all."

"I know very well my circumstances," Grace said, standing and walking with a straight back to the piano. She let her fingers trail over a few keys, starting a hopeful tune. "Grace Marie Haggerty, 26, elder sister of Patricia Haggerty Owens, piano teacher and spinster." With the last word, Grace banged her fist into the lowest notes.

"Grace, I—I know it's been hard for you all these years. Why, you've been the picture of sweetness to me, even when Charles proposed and you were my maid of honor. I can't help it if I want you to be as happy as I am. Surely there will be several eligible bachelors not from around here at the dinner. Someone who won't mind—"

"Let me finish that for you," Grace said. "Someone who won't mind marrying a woman who can't have children. There. It's not so hard to say, is it?"

"Someone older, possibly, someone who maybe already has grown children..." Patty played along, encouraging her sister.

"Someone who doesn't need money, or a family. Yes, someone who wants a soon-to-be old maid. I'm sure there will plenty of men like that."

"Well!" Patty said. "If you're going to take that attitude, I can see why no man would look twice at you." Why couldn't Grace see that Patty only had her best interests at heart? Surely being married to a man—even one who didn't marry you for love—was better than sitting by yourself night after night, teaching other people's children to play the piano?

It pained Grace to see Patty trying to be cross. Her sister couldn't stay mad at anyone long. But the only thing worse than having her sister try to set her up with eligible men, was the complete lack of invitations she had received for the past year. Turning 26 and having her younger sister marry ahead of her had pushed her off all of the social calendars. The fact of her illness that had left her unable to have children just sealed her fate.

"Oh, everyone knows everything in this town anyway!" Grace said, smiling at Patty. "It might be a fun time. I'll go with you."

Patty clapped her hands like a small child. "I knew it! I knew you couldn't resist me. Now, what have you got to wear? Show me everything and I can lend you one of these new hats..." Patty started up the stairs to Grace's room.

"I'll be right there," Grace said. She picked up the newspaper sticking out of Patty's shopping basket. It was folded open to the Society Page, where Patty kept track of all the important matters to her in Hopewell Township, New Jersey.

A small advertisement caught her eye. *Looking for Love? Find it in The Matrimonial Gazette! On Newsstands Now – only 5¢.* She squinted a little and took it under the lamp. *Nationwide distribution—Women's Ads Free.*

"Grace! This blue one will do nicely! Do come up and bring the hats with you!"

"Coming!" Grace called. She took the Society Page and put it among her sheet music on the piano. *I'll go to the dinner. But there's no reason not to take matters in to my own hands.*

She rushed up the stairs to join Patty. *The sooner she's satisfied, the sooner I can be alone. I've got an advertisement to write.*

3

Chapter Four

Annabelle could hardly wait for supper. She pestered Loretta long enough that the old housekeeper finally sat down and fixed her hair in "fancy" braids, pulling the long pieces out from her face and back, plaiting them against her head on both sides leading down to bright blue ribbons on the blonde ends.

Willie, on the other hand, had to be practically wrestled into his good trousers and shirt.

"If ever the Lord made two more different children, born of the same parents and at the same time, I've never seen it!" Loretta exclaimed in exasperation as she finished buttoning his collar. He wriggled and squirmed away from her. "William! You sit right here and let me comb that hair."

At the sound of his full name, Willie scowled and crossed his arms. He shook his head, *No*, brown curls tossing about his face.

"Oh, no, Loretta! He's crossed his arms." Annabelle said. "You better wait a bit before combing his hair. Here, Willie, can I brush it with my soft brush? It doesn't pull the tangles as much."

Loretta left the room, muttering under her breath that Mrs. Thompkins would never see fit to have them in school, much less take them as her own.

Annabelle smiled at Willie. She twirled around and her braids flew out from her head. "What do you think, Willie? Will Father like my hair?"

Willie kept scowling, but he let go of one arm. His hand slipped into his pocket and toyed with something. He could never resist a smile from Annabelle for long, and eventually his face broke into a shy grin.

She rushed over and gave him a hug. "You'll see," she said. "School will be fun. And Mrs. Thompkins will know right away how smart you are. You read twice as fast as I do. I see you finishing my books while I'm still reading them."

Willie smiled and nodded. He pulled his hand out of his pocket and opened it to Annabelle.

She looked down and he pushed his hand closer to her.

"Mama's comb!" she said. "Willie, where did you find it?"

Willie closed his eyes. He brought his hand to his heart, holding the comb over it. He bent his head and kissed it in his hand, then opened it back up toward Annabelle.

She reached out with trembling fingers, held it up to one side of her head, and slid the teeth between strands of her hair. She looked up at Willie.

His smile was as wide as the hills.

"Will you let me brush your hair now?" Annabelle said softly.

He nodded his head, *Yes*.

Annabelle took the brush and gently tugged it through his wild hair. When she was finished, she smiled at him in the mirror. Her straight blonde braids and his curly brown hair were opposite, but the two sets of brown eyes that smiled at each other in the mirror were exactly the same.

Willie stood and took Annabelle's hand as they walked downstairs to the sound of Will Forrester greeting his guests.

"My dear Mr. Forrester!" A woman's loud voice floated out of the entranceway and up the stairs. Willie hesitated, but Annabelle tugged on his hand and kept going.

"Mrs. Thompkins! Come in, come in. Lovely to see you." Will greeted her warmly. The children watched as he took her hand and kissed her cheek. He leaned back from the kiss, and Miss Thompkins resolutely turned her other cheek toward him. He hesitated, then leaned in awkwardly and quickly pecked the other side.

"Ha ha, yes that's it! Just like the French, you know! So very sophisticated to kiss both cheeks, don't you think?"

"Ahem," Will said, averting his eyes. "Mr. Busby, so glad you could come," he said. A short, stout gentleman shook Will's hand. He smiled and the tips of his handlebar mustache rose with his cheeks.

"Good to see you, old man," Mr. Busby said. "Glad to know you're doing well, doing very well indeed."

"My, this is a handsome entrance!" Miss Thompkins said. She stood nearly as tall as Will, at 5 feet 10 inches. With her square shoulders, cinched waist, and large bustle, she was a study in angles and shapes. She placed her hands on her hips, elbows out, and looked around with her nose in the air, as if she were sniffing something. She spied the children shrunk back against the large walnut post at the bottom of the banister.

"There you are! Hiding right there on the steps. Come forward, children!"

Will, somewhat stunned at her grand entrance, came to life. "Willie, Annabelle, come here now. Miss Thompkins, I'd like you to meet my children, Willie and Annabelle." The children crept forward and stood, one on each side of their father. Miss Thompkins lowered her chin somewhat, but still peered down at them from the full length of her sharp nose.

"How do you do, Annabelle," she said, extending a limp hand. Annabelle stepped forward and took her hand, giving it a slight shake.

"I'm very pleased to meet you, Miss Thompkins." She gave a small curtsy.

"Charming! And William, so very much like your father. How do you do?"

Willie's eyes blazed out at the sound of his formal name, but his father gave him a gentle shove forward. He reached for the hand offered him, took it briefly, and bowed, before stepping back one pace behind his father.

"Ah, a quiet one, I see. Well, that will change when I call on you in school, you can count on it! Now Will, do show me about, I simply love learning the history of a home." Miss Thompkins put her hand up and held it there until Will offered her his arm. They strolled off together into the parlor, Mr. Busby trailing behind, and Will pointing out the woodwork as she exclaimed over the furnishings.

Loretta poked her head out of the kitchen door and hissed, "I thought there were two more coming? Anybody on the porch?"

Willie jumped to the window and peered out before turning to shake his head at her.

"Just the five of you, then. Well, I suppose this extra food will keep for leftovers, I never can tell how much I'm supposed to make..." She ducked back into the kitchen.

Willie and Annabelle exchanged glances as if to say, "What do you think?" They shrugged their shoulders and wrinkled their noses at each other, then burst out giggling.

"What's this? Private joking when company is present is the height of incivility," Miss Thompkins said as she and Will appeared back in the foyer.

"The children understand each other in a way no one else does," Will explained. "Been that way since they were born."

"Hmmm. Yes, twins, I see," Miss Tompkins said. "Well, we shall see if they can be separated into separate classrooms. The school is growing, you know! Why, I wouldn't be surprised if we had three first grade classes this year! It's always the largest with students coming in, until we see who can be moved ahead."

"But Willie and I want to stay together," Annabelle began, but a look from her father silenced her.

Willie was beginning to scowl, but Annabelle whispered, "Don't worry. We'll make out the same on our exams, and she'll have no choice but to keep us together." He nodded as they walked behind their father, Miss Thompkins and Mr. Busby into the dining room.

"What an ... interesting ... choice of wallpaper," Miss Thompkins said as Will held out her chair at one end of the table. "Large flowers and greenery. Fine for its day, but a bit dated for my tastes."

Now Annabelle began to scowl. The wallpaper in the dining room had been her mother's favorite. She, Willie and her father knew it. No one said a word.

The children spent the rest of the meal following Loretta's training to only speak when spoken to. It suited Willie just fine to keep his thoughts to himself, but Annabelle was nearly exploding by the time the meal was over. Miss Thompkins spoke only to Will and Mr. Busby, as if the children weren't even there. When Annabelle had something she wanted to say, she opened her mouth and looked at her father. He shook his head at her, and she clamped her lips back shut.

"Well, now!" Will said as Loretta came in with the coffee pot. "Children, you may be excused while we I finish our coffee."

"Thank you, Father," Annabelle said. "Excuse me, Miss Thompkins, Mr. Busby." She stood and laid her napkin on the table beside her plate and looked at Willie.

On cue, he rose and smiled at Will, then turned and half-bowed again to Miss Thompkins. Napkin in hand, he was about to walk away.

"Aren't you going to ask to be excused, William?" Miss Tompkins said.

"Oh, he did ask—" Annabelle said.

"I certainly didn't hear him. William?"

Willie's hand holding the napkin came forward and crossed his body. His other arm began its ascent to meet the elbow on the other side. Before his stance could solidify, Will broke in.

"It's all right, Miss Thompkins. You may not have heard him, but Willie communicated his request to me just fine. Willie, you're excused.

"Willie? Is that a proper name for a boy from a fine family? Will, I implore you, treat the children with a bit more decorum, and others will respect them as well. I, for one, prefer a full Christian name, such as William—" She stopped as even she noticed the look on Will's face. "Or Will, of course ...."

Annabelle and Willie mercifully heard no more as they escaped back upstairs. They couldn't get out of range of Miss Thompkins' voice fast enough.

"Poor father!" Annabelle said as soon as they were alone in their room. "Having to entertain Miss Thompkins, just because he wants us to go to school!"

Willie took the napkin still in his hand and threw it on the ground. He stomped it with his foot for good measure.

They put on their nightclothes and slipped into adjoining twin beds. They lay quietly in the dark for a long time, until they heard the sound of their father opening the door. Then they both pretended to be asleep.

Will Forrester came in and leaned over each child to give them a kiss good night. He thought he saw Annabelle smile in her sleep. *So much like my Anna.* He leaned over Willie and saw his son was breathing a bit fast. He put his hand on Willie's forehead and the boy's eyes opened.

"Thank you for keeping your temper at the table, Willie," Will said. "I hope you'll grow to like Miss Thompkins. We may be seeing a lot more of her."

Willie's round brown eyes looked up at his father in the dark. He slowly shook his head, *No.*

Will touched his hand to his son's check. "Go to sleep, now," he said. Then he got up and quietly closed the door. He walked down the hallway to his room, went in and sat for a long while at the chair by the window.

SHE'S CERTAINLY NOTHING LIKE ANNA, Will thought to himself. Then he hung his head. He'd had his one love in this life, and she'd been taken from him. Now it was up to him to raise their children with the most love and best education he could give them.

Besides, Miss Thompkins was a good conversationalist, well-travelled and certainly well-regarded in town. He could use a bit more socializing.

The first year after Anna died was the hardest. Every week, every month, held a new anniversary of the fact that she wasn't there. It had been a full two years now, and he had to admit he was lonely. Cutting up with Loretta and talking to the other famers was about the most he could manage on most days. Annabelle was his little chatterbox, and she was great company, but Willie—no, it was Willie who worried him the most.

He's carrying the burden that I alone bear. I should have been there to protect Anna. I should have been the last one in the cellar.

Will allowed his mind to go back to remember the look of panic on Willie's face when he had returned to the farm at the tail end of the storm. "I held onto her, I tried!" Willie had said. But when they found Anna's lifeless body in a field, Willie had sobbed bitter tears, but not said another word since. Both father and son felt they had let each other down.

Harriet is my best hope, Will thought. *I've given him all the love I can. Maybe a little sternness will snap him out of this.*

He didn't believe it in his heart, but his head convinced him he had to try something.

Chapter Five

*W*illie woke up before Annabelle with a feeling of dread in the pit of his stomach. He rubbed and pushed on his belly but it wouldn't go away. Annabelle was still asleep, so he got up quietly, slipped on his trousers and shirt, and headed downstairs.

Sounds of Loretta starting the fire in the stove came from the kitchen. *I should check the wood box.* But he was drawn instead to his father's low humming coming from the study.

Will Forrester was at his desk, going over his books for the farm. He looked up when Willie appeared next to him.

"Good morning! Come here and give me a hug."

Willie put his arms around Will's neck and climbed up into his lap. He looked at the record book laid open in front of him.

"Here's where I write in weekly expenses," his father said. "And here's where I put in the price I've gotten for our crops."

Willie stared at the figures. He could read the words, but didn't yet understand the numbers.

"When you go to school, you'll learn how to add and subtract big columns like this."

Willie looked at him with wide eyes.

"Of course, not at first! Don't worry, you'll start with two at a time. One day, you'll help me and take over all this figuring."

Willie smiled.

"I have to go into town today, would you like to come with me? I noticed you could use a haircut."

Willie jumped off his father's lap and headed for the door.

"I'll take that as a 'Yes.' Let me get my hat." Will put his arm around Willie's shoulder, and the two walked out to the barn to hitch up the horse to the wagon.

"Going somewhere without me?" Annabelle called from the bedroom window. "Wait! I want to come!"

She got dressed as quickly as she could and ran downstairs and out onto the porch. Will pulled up and Willie reached out to give Annabelle a hand up into the cart.

They drove to town, enjoying the fresh morning air, the birds singing, and the sun rising higher in the sky. The only thing not restful was Annabelle peppering her father with questions.

"Do you really like Miss Thompkins, Father? She seemed awfully stiff to me."

"She is used to being an example in front of children. I'm sure you'll like her more once you get to know her."

"But do you like her?"

"I do like her. She's smart, and from one of the best families in town. She loves children …"

"I'm not so sure about that."

"Really? Why?"

"She didn't understand Willie at all."

"Well, it's a bit hard to understand someone who isn't saying anything. You'll see, going to school will help Willie. He'll want to talk to the teacher and the other children. He'll learn a lot and won't be able to keep it inside."

Willie bounced along beside Annabelle, listening to every word.

Annabelle wrestled with asking the question she was most worried about. She finally blurted out: "Loretta says you may want to marry Miss Thompkins."

Will Forrester shook his head. He'd wanted to begin this conversation himself with the children, but now that the question was out in the open, he had to answer her directly. He pulled the horse to a stop in front of the barber shop. A few men sat outside playing checkers in the shade. Will kept his voice low.

"Annabelle. Willie. I've thought very hard about this. It's time we had a woman in the house to take care of things and help raise you properly. You two aren't getting any younger, and neither am I. We could do a lot worse than Miss Thompkins."

Annabelle sat with her mouth open. "I didn't believe Loretta," she finally said.

Willie jumped out of the cart. He held his hand over his eyes to shade them from the sun and looked up at his father. He shook his head slowly from left to right. *No.*

"I'll decide who I marry when the time is right," Will said. "Come on, let's see about cleaning you up a bit."

ANNABELLE AND WILLIE SAT together in chairs along the side of the barber shop, watching Old Sam shave their father's face. The two men playing checkers outside came in chuckling over a newspaper.

"It says right here, 'Husband Wanted.' I tell you, Will, this is your chance!" said Tom.

"Hee hee!" hooted Cal. "You can have your pick!" The men continued reading the ads from The Matrimonial Gazette.

"What kind of paper is that, anyway?" said Old Sam.

"A new one!" said Tom. "Just came in to the mercantile. It's mostly full of men looking for wives. But this here section is all about the ladies!"

"Read another 'un," Old Sam said.

"Ok, here goes," said Tom. "Former dancer available for eligible man for proper marriage offers only. Hard worker, physically fit, attractive. Age 39 but look like 35."

"Haw haw! She's the right age for you, Will!" Cal said, bending over with laughter.

Old Sam tried to keep a straight face and a steady razor, but he had to stop shaving and step back to keep his hand from nicking Will's face. "Go on, enough of that, now! I got work to do!"

Tom and Cal took their leave. "This'll be right here for the next fella, then." Tom said, dropping the paper on a chair. "Don't say we didn't try to help you out."

Annabelle and Willie looked at each other. They couldn't tell their father's reaction underneath the shaving cream covering half his face. They nodded, and both stood up at the same time. Willie moved toward the empty barber's chair next to his father, signaling he was ready for his turn. Old Sam smiled at him and kept his attention on Will's face.

Annabelle stood in front of the chair holding the paper. She bent her knees slightly until her fingers touched the edge, then she clutched it behind her back. "Think I'll go say hello to Mrs. Fuller at the mercantile," she said.

"All right, honey," said Will, his face now clean. "Won't take long to snip off Will's curls."

Annabelle rushed out and down the street to be alone with the paper. By the time she, her father and Willie were back on the cart riding home, she knew what to do.

～ჰ～

"THIS IS HER. SHE'S THE ONE," Annabelle said, pointing to Grace's ad. Willie read over her shoulder, his lips moving silently as he read the words.

"Cultured woman, age 26, interested in marriage partnership with gentleman who reads, writes, and enjoys music. Quiet, educated piano teacher who can cook, keep house and entertain. Cannot promise children, but younger widowers with children considered."

He nodded his head solemnly as he sat in his father's desk chair, pen in hand.

"Write it in capital letters," Annabelle said. "You can keep them straight that way. Maybe she'll think Father works for the telegraph office."

Willie concentrated on the paper, ready to take dictation.

"Dear Miss Haggerty," Annabelle said. "That's Hag, H-A-G; gerty, G-E-R-T-Y. Got it?

Willie nodded his head as he formed the print capital letters.

"I am a widower with a boy and a girl." Annabelle paused so Willie could catch up. "I live on a nice farm in Fair Isle, Iowa."

"I offer you a place in my family as my wife." Annabelle stopped. "Oh dear … should I say that?"

Willie nodded. He straightened his shoulders and looked down his nose at Annabelle.

"You're right—otherwise, it'll be Miss Thompkins for sure. Ok, keep writing: Please come as soon as you can. I will pay for the ticket when you get here. Yours truly, William Forrester." There—do you have all that?"

Willie nodded but kept slowly writing. When he finished, Annabelle read it over before folding it, addressing the envelope and finding a stamp. She smiled as she read Willie's ending.

"P.S. We like music."

Chapter Six

Grace stood at the postmaster's office, stunned by the pile of letters he had for her.

"I can't imagine how you've gotten so popular so fast," Mr. Goff said. "Must be lots of pen pals."

"Yes ... must be," Grace said. "Thank you." She turned away and hurried out before Mr. Goff could ask any more questions.

Wonderful. It's not enough that I was humiliated at the Princeton club dinner, now Mr. Goff will be telling everyone how much mail I'm getting! Grace thought as she made her way back home. *I've got to pick from one of these. I pray I make the right choice.*

She slipped inside and went to the kitchen where the light streamed in the window. She took the letters and made piles according to states: 7 from Colorado, 4 from Montana, 5 from Nebraska, and 2 from Iowa.

Eighteen! Surely there's a gentleman among them. She opened the letters from Colorado and Montana first, but quickly realized the hard life they described would be more than she wanted to endure. She went through the letters from Nebraska next. She made two new piles, one for possibilities and the rest for rejects. She didn't have much to go on, but counted poor spelling and grammar against them, all else being equal. Most asked straight out if she could have children, when she clearly stated in her ad (well, maybe hinted) that she could not.

Finally, she had two letters in the possibilities pile. One from a dentist in Nebraska who sounded very nice. The other from a farmer in Fair Isle, Iowa. She couldn't tell much at all by his letter. In fact, it was written more like a telegraph in the oddest handwriting.

He can certainly spell, so he must be educated; he just has poor penmanship. But he does have two children, so should be fine with not having any more. How old does it say he is? Oh, he doesn't say.

She turned again to the letter from Nebraska. There. The dentist was 38, at least he wasn't too old. She searched through the letters, trying to read between the lines. The dentist seemed like he'd be happy with a long correspondence before deciding to visit. She re-read the letter from Fair Isle:

Please come as soon as you can. ... P.S. We like music. Here was someone who needed her, and he had read her ad well enough to know she was a piano teacher.

She took up a pen to reply.

Dear Mr. Forrester.

I shall come as soon as possible to Fair Isle. I will be glad to make your acquaintance and those of your two children. I will bring my music sheets with me.

Yours Truly,

Grace Haggerty

She bundled up the rest of the letters and threw them one by one into the fire. She left immediately to go buy her train ticket and to tell Mr. Goff to send all her mail back, return to sender. She'd stop by Patty's after she was packed and on her way to the station. She wanted to say good-bye, but she didn't want any chance she could be talked out of it.

She put on her hat and stood at the door, looking around the parlor. No, she wouldn't miss this place. Too many good-byes at the door with no one to talk to in the morning or evening. She walked over to the piano and looked through her sheet music. She picked her favorites, old and new, classical and more recent songs of the Civil War and patriotism. She had one or two comical tunes. She stopped when she came to the new National hymn.

This will be a rousing tune and something I can teach the children:

> *My Country! tis of thee,*
>
> *Sweet land of liberty*
>
> *Of thee I sing;*
>
> *Land where my fathers died,*
>
> *Land of the Pilgrims' pride.*

From every mountain side

Let freedom ring.

There. She smiled, put on her hat, and hurried to set her plans in place.

Chapter Seven

W ill Forrester was confused. He'd received a cryptic letter from a woman he'd never met, saying she would be there – when was it? As soon as possible? *Maybe Loretta knows what this is about.*

He went to the kitchen to find her, but as he passed the staircase, heard her voice upstairs talking to the children as she made the beds. The clock on the mantel struck 11. *This will have to wait.*

He had promised to take Harriet on a picnic, and had a strong feeling it would start off badly if he was late.

As Will drove to town, he tried to reason with himself that this was the right decision. Annabelle needed a mother, and Willie couldn't go on much longer without finding his voice again. The doctor had cautioned that trauma like Willie had experienced had unexpected effects on young children. But the sooner life could return to normal, the sooner he'd return to his former self.

Only life had gone on, if not normally, at least in a new sort of reality. And still, Willie seemed more comfortable just letting Annabelle speak for him. Will knew he had to do something soon.

Harriet was waiting for him at the door. "I thought maybe you'd forgotten what day it was!" she exclaimed, trying to sound light but her annoyance creeping through.

Will checked his pocket watch. "It's just now 11, did I get the time wrong?"

"No, but as I always tell the students, 'If you're not five minutes early, you're bound to be late'."

The warm feelings Will had been trying to cultivate started to get a little worn down at the rebuke. He pulled the horse away from the house, all conversational thoughts driven from his mind by the way Harriet talked. Lots of statements and pronouncements; not very many questions.

He pulled up to the spot near an old oak tree and they walked through the field. When they got under the shade of the tree, Harriet spread out a tablecloth she had brought and they both sat on opposite edges of it with the basket between them.

Harriet was 32, just a year younger than Will, though her demeanor was of a much older woman. "I hope you like cold cuts and biscuits. I bought a pie last week also. I don't have much time to cook, you know."

"I don't imagine you do," said Will, although he wondered, with school out, why she didn't have more time.

"Every summer it's the same thing," said Harriet. "First we have to clean and rearrange the school rooms. Then I always have to interview for new teachers – every year someone gets married and gives up the profession. I would never do that!"

"What, get married?"

"No, of course I fully expect to marry," Harriet said. She realized her voice had been a bit strident, so she curved her mouth up into a smile and tried batting her eyelashes at him.

Has she got something in her eye? Will thought. He was just about to offer her his handkerchief when her eyelids stopped opening and closing so fast. Her smile faded.

"I just do not intend to give up my position," she continued. "I've worked too long and too hard to become the headmistress. It's a job very few women can earn, and I don't want to disappoint the school board."

"No, of course not. Say, do you feel that Annabelle and Willie are ready for school? Anna was able to teach them to read and Loretta helps them with handwriting. I was hoping soon they would learn mathematics and science; you know, all the subjects."

"I daresay they are more than ready," Harriet said. "The longer they're kept to their own devices, the wilder they get. Children's minds must be molded, you know! And their characters!"

Will nodded and tried to take a bite of the tough biscuit. He gave up and hid it behind him when Harriet wasn't looking.

"What will become of our society if children aren't educated? And trained?" Harriet continued.

"I'm sure parents have a lot to do with how well children turn out. That's why I've gotten more interested lately in finding a wife who can also be a loving mother for the twins." Will searched her face. Could this woman have any motherly instincts at all?

"They are attractive, for children," Harriet said stiffly. "I mean, I do truly love children, Will."

She moved her hand a bit closer towards him. He reached for it and looked into her eyes.

"Harriet, do you think it would be too forward of me..."

"Why, I believe forthright honesty is the bedrock of all relationships."

"All right then. Would you consider an engagement, a long one, so we can get to know each other better? I won't stand in the way of your position at the school. And it will give Annabelle and Willie a chance to get used to the idea."

Harriet had begun smiling when Will made his proposal, but couldn't hide the disdain in her voice at his bringing the twins into it. "Children have no business influencing their parent's decisions," she said.

"That may be," Will said. "But they've been through a lot – we all have. And since Anna's death, I've relied on their love and support almost as much as I did hers. I feel I owe it to them."

"We'll see," Harriet said. "I consent to your proposal, but I ask that our decision to finalize our nuptials be strictly between us. I couldn't abide coming in to the home in a lesser position to the children."

"I wouldn't allow it," Will said. He reached forward and Harriet offered him her cheek. He kissed it, catching a faint whiff of moth balls covered up with rose water. Something turned in his stomach.

"Shall we pack up then, Will? I'm anxious to return to my duties."

"Yes, Harriet. I'll call on you again soon and have you to the house. Once the children know you are my fiancé, I'm sure everything will be fine."

"It matters not, am I correct?"

Will pretended he didn't hear her as he put the picnic basket into the wagon. *This doesn't feel like the butterflies I remember, but*

I'm sure Harriet will be a good influence on Willie and Annabelle.

Chapter Eight

race loved all the scenery and towns on her trip from New Jersey. She had spent the time moving to a different car each day to meet new travelers and keep from being bored. She had a map in her reticule, and had Fair Isle circled on it. She couldn't believe it was time to meet her potential new husband.

At the station, she asked the station master if she could leave her large trunk there until she could hire a cart.

"I can hire one for you," he said. "Where are you headed?"

"I was hoping I could walk," she said. "I'm going to the Forrester farm. Is it far out of town?"

"About three miles. Are you sure?" The man looked at her over his glasses.

"I'm quite sure! It's not so very hot out, and my legs are cramped from days on the train. I like to get a feel for a place when I visit, and the best way I know is to walk."

He pointed her in the right direction, and Grace set off. She left Station Street and turned onto Main Street, enjoying the storefronts and business she passed. She walked by a large, red brick building that looked like the school. A tall man was helping a broad-shouldered woman out of a wagon, and handing her a picnic basket. They stood on the sidewalk for a moment together.

How quaint! Grace thought, averting her eyes as she strolled quickly by. She turned her head slightly after she passed in time to see the two kiss each other – on both cheeks. *Very cosmopolitan!*

Grace left the town behind and continued down a dirt road lined with a white pasture fence. Some fields had horses and cows in them, but there were rows and rows of crops, from beans to squash to tall, green corn. She had never seen so many fields stretching far off into the distance, with only a few houses and barns in between. The land was certainly bigger and less populated in Iowa.

Her legs felt good walking along, but her arms and shoulders were feeling the strain of hauling along her reticule. She kept moving it from one side to the other, but each time she could go fewer steps before she had to move it back. She finally came to a crossroad, which by the station master's directions was the last one before the Forrester farm, and sat down in some shade to rest.

"Come on! You can do it!" A little girl's voice rose out from behind Grace's perch. "You used to swim with Mama all the time! Come on, Willie!"

The girl continued to yell, but Grace heard no reply in return. Curious, she got up and followed the sound of the voice until she heard splashing water. She stepped through the rows of corn, and saw a wide pond open up before her. A girl was splashing and diving around, occasionally coming to the surface to call to a small child sitting on a log.

"You must be hot – I know you are! Just put your toes in! I won't splash you – promise!"

Grace saw the boy shake his head vigorously and pull his feet under him, as if to resist the temptation to cool them off.

"Hello, there!" she called. "Mind if I join you?" Grace came to the log and put out her hand. "Grace Haggerty, and my feet could use some cooling off. Do you mind?"

Willie looked up at her in astonishment. He looked to the water, but Annabelle hadn't seen or heard the newcomer. He stood and seemed as if he was going to shout, but changed his mind.

"Well, I'll just stay a little bit," Grace said. She sat down and unbuckled first one shoe, then the other. She removed her stockings and rolled them up inside her shoes.

"Hello! I didn't see you there!" called Annabelle from the water. The little girl came to the edge of the pond, the mud under her feet making a sucking sound. "Are you coming swimming?"

"Not swimming, no," Grace said. "My name's Grace. What's yours."

"Grace! Grace Haggerty?" Annabelle shrieked. "Willie, did you hear? She's come!"

Willie nodded and smiled.

"You were expecting me, then," said Grace. "Are you the Forrester children?"

"The very ones!" Annabelle said, laughing. She stood dripping wet at the edge of the pond. "I'm Annabelle, and this is Willie. He loves to swim, but won't do it anymore, ever since – "

"Very nice to meet you, Annabelle, Willie," said Grace, shaking their hands. "Willie, would you steady me while I step in? I don't want to lose my footing in the mud."

Willie didn't have a chance to step back. Grace held on to his shoulder and put one foot down into the water. She slipped a little and Annabelle and Willie both reached for her. She put her hand up.

"It's all right, I think I've got it. Ahhh. Didn't realize how lovely it would be to cool my toes."

Soon Annabelle was back splashing in the water, and Grace held up her skirts and explored around the edges. Willie walked along beside her, happy as she commented on a firefly or unusual rock. Grace looked at him and smiled.

"Would you like to join us?"

Willie nodded. He stripped off his shirt, and took a running leap into the pond, nearly sinking Annabelle and covering Grace with a spray of water.

"Willie! You did it!" Annabelle was beaming. Soon the two of them were diving and blowing bubbles and Grace found a rock at water's edge to sit on.

A large crash through the cornstalks interrupted them.

"Willie! Annabelle!" said Will. "I asked you not to swim when I'm not home, who knows what might happen –"

He stopped when he saw Grace. She took one look at him – the same man she had seen in town kissing the woman – took a step back, slipped, and fell with a loud splash into the pond.

Chapter Nine

*W*ill could not believe his eyes. Annabelle – and Willie – were laughing and swimming in the pond! Willie wouldn't go swimming last summer, and it seemed as if he would stay on the sideline again this summer. But somehow, this woman was standing there watching both his children swim. *Who was she?*

He rushed to the edge of the pond and reached out his hand to help her up. She was sputtering, and had lost most of her hairpins and all of her dignity. Her long brown locks were dripping down her face and neck. She avoided his eyes, but took his hand as he pulled her upright and back to the safety of the water's edge.

"Miss! Are you hurt? I hope you are not injured!"

Grace couldn't help laughing at his manners. "I am not injured, except for my pride. Oh my, I must look dreadful. My hair! And my dress! I was only just cooling off my feet ..."

"Father! Father! Look at Willie!" Annabelle said.

Willie waved and did a half dive under water, coming up behind Annabelle and giving her a hug. The two clambered to the edge and crawled up onto the grass, rolling in it and laughing.

"Father, this is Grace Haggerty! She's come to stay!"

Will remembered the letter he had received. Was she there as a governess? Maybe Harriet had placed an advertisement, thinking it would be a help for him with the children.

"Are you an acquaintance of Miss Thompkins, then?" Will asked, shaking Grace's hand.

"N-no, but I think I know who you're speaking of," Grace said. She thought back on the sharp-nosed woman she had seen Will kissing. "Is she your fiancée?"

The children stopped pushing each other and stared at Will. "What? You've asked her? Father!" said Annabelle.

Grace raised one eyebrow and looked into Will's face. His eyes were brown under deep, thick eyebrows. His square jaw made him seem a bit rough, but already the concern in his voice even as he scolded the children showed her that his was a kind soul.

He looked at her painfully, then turned to Annabelle.

"I-I've something to tell you," he said slowly. "Miss Thompkins and I just today have become engaged. But Miss Haggerty, if Harriet didn't send for you, who did?"

Annabelle and Willie had begun stepping away from the edge of the pond, clothes in hand, toward the cornfield and back to the road.

"Wait! Annabelle? Willie!" Will yelled.

The children took off running.

"It's my fault entirely," Grace said. "I should have known by the writing – my goodness, I did wonder about it. And yet –"

Will was utterly confused. Grace took one look at his incredulous expression and spilled out everything she knew.

"I took out an advertisement, you see; well, I'd never done anything like it before. But every day of my life had become all the same. No, to be perfectly honest, each day was getting worse. I couldn't stay in Hopewell Township any longer. When I received your letter – I mean, the children's letter – saying to come right away ... I confess I was entirely and uncharacteristically hasty. I should never have come until I corresponded with you..."

Will's face went from surprise to shock. He looked up at the sky and closed his eyes. His chin shook in a small motion left to right. Slowly, the grimace on his face broke into grin, and he put his hands on either side of his head.

"Those rascals! What am I going to do? Miss Haggerty –"

"Please," she said, pointing to her wet gown. "Under the circumstances, call me Grace."

"Grace – what can I say? I have two of the wildest children in the county, if not the state! How dare they impersonate me! And to think you've come all this way, for nothing –"

Grace had been smiling as Will described with such obvious love what his children had done.

But at the word "nothing," her face fell.

"I saw you with Miss Thompkins, in town," she said. "I won't make any trouble for you. It's all been an unfortunate misunderstanding. I can see you would never answer an advertisement for a bride. Now if you'll excuse me, I'll get my things and head back to town before dark. I'll leave in the morning."

Her polite withdrawal sent Will's mind spinning. He wanted to scream and shout. Her voice, her smiling eyes, her hair, even wet – everything about her sent his stomach into somersaults. She smelled like warm sunshine, and cool water, and he loved it.

And somehow, she had gotten Willie to swim.

"No, Grace. Please. It's late, and you've travelled a long way. Please, come to the house, get dried off and cleaned up, and have something to eat. It's the least I can do. We'll clear everything up in the morning."

Grace nodded her head and sat down to put on her shoes. He watched her silently, then followed behind as she made her way back to the road and his waiting horse cart.

Chapter Ten

"I .tell you, a woman has enough work to do, and she looks away for one minute, and do you see what happens? You children had clean clothes on and were freshly bathed yesterday. And you come traipsin' up to my door, all wet and muddy! And Annabelle! Your hair! Child, were you rolling in the mud?"

Loretta kept up a steady pace of complaints and questions. The twins were mortified when she made them strip down to their undergarments on the back porch, and stand and wait while she scrubbed down first one, and then the other, in the washtub.

"Ouch! You're too rough!" Annabelle complained.

"Never you mind! How else can I get this dirt off of your arms and legs? I can't understand how a body could get this dirty from swimming!"

Willie giggled watching Annabelle take the brunt of Loretta's aggravation, only to find out her strength hadn't faded when it was his turn. He squirmed and wiggled away from her strong hands and the rough cloth she was scrubbing him with.

"Now stand still, or I'll tie you to a chair in the tub!" she said.

Willie stood still, but stuck out his tongue at Annabelle when she started laughing at him from under the towel she was using to dry her hair.

"Now go on up and get in your Sunday clothes! That's right! I'm not washing extra play clothes because you two decide to wallow in the dirt! You can just sit around the house like proper folk for the rest of the day!"

Annabelle and Willie got away from her as fast as they were able, and ran up to their room.

Loretta was dumping out the dirty wash water when Will and Grace pulled up. Will helped Grace down from the cart, and brought her up to the back door.

"I'm afraid you'll need to heat some more water, Loretta," he said. "Miss Grace Haggerty, this is Miss Loretta Potter. Loretta, do you mind helping Grace find something clean to wear? Oh, and put an extra plate outr?"

Loretta's mouth hung open for a second. "Nice to meet you, Miss Haggerty."

"Please, call me Grace. And I can pour my own water, and help you with the meal. Just give me a few moments to get cleaned up."

"Yes, well, I'll leave you two ladies then," said Will uncomfortably, and he strode off toward the barn.

As Grace washed, Loretta went to Anna's trunk and found a dress that would fit. She put it in the spare bedroom and showed Grace the way.

"Here you are. Just let me know if you need anything," Loretta said.

"I'm fine. I have my traveling case in my reticule and – Oh! This is a lovely dress."

"It was Miss Anna's," Loretta said. "I think it was one of Mr. Forrester's favorites." She smiled.

Grace looked at her in surprise, then nodded her head. "If you think I should," she said.

"Oh, I do," said Loretta. "Somebody's got to get through to that man's heart, and I believe you might be the one to do it. Least get his mind off marrying Miss Thompkins." Loretta shivered. "That woman could raise a squirrel out of winter hibernation with her voice!" She winked, and closed the door.

Grace burst out laughing, and hurried to change and finish drying her hair. She wanted to explore the house before supper.

She walked down the upstairs hallway, peeking into open rooms. Willie and Annabelle lay napping on their beds in clean undergarments, having fallen asleep rather than get dressed in their Sunday clothes. She passed the open door to the main bedroom at the end of the hall, using all her will power not to look in as she started down the stairs.

On the main level of the house to her right was a large room with a pine table and chairs, a china cabinet, and a serving board. To her left was the parlor. She spied a piano in the corner, covered in a sheet to keep off the dust. She walked over, pulled up the sheet to reveal the keys, and sat down.

She played quietly at first, to calm her own nerves and avoid waking the children. In a few minutes, she was lost in her music, until she felt two warm breaths on either side of her.

Annabelle and Willie stood next to her in their Sunday clothes. Willie's shirt was buttoned crookedly, and the ribbon on Anna's dress hung untied down to the floor. She stopped playing.

"Can you keep going?" Annabelle said. "That was beautiful."

Grace thought of all the children she had taught to play back in Hopewell Township, and which songs they asked her to play most often.

"I've got a new one for you. Would you like to hear it?"

"Yes, please!" said Annabelle.

Willie nodded his head, *Yes*.

"All right. It moves along pretty fast but you can sing the chorus with me. Here goes:"

Camptown ladies sing this song, doo-dah, doo-dah

Camptown racetrack's five miles long, oh doo-dah day

Goin' to run all night! Goin' to run all day!

I bet my money on a bobtail nag, somebody bet on the bay

Annabelle clapped her hands. "That's a fun one! Play it again!"

By the time Grace played the song three or four more times, the children were clapping and Annabelle was loudly singing along with Grace. None of them heard Will's footsteps as he came into the parlor.

"What's this?"

Grace's fingers abruptly stopped, but Annabelle carried on, "*Oh, doo-dah day!* Father, isn't it fun? I love this song!"

"It's a lively one, all right. I'm not sure it's quite appropriate for your age..."

"It's perfectly harmless," said Grace. "I only picked it because I can remember how to play it, and all of my sheet music is in my trunk back in town."

"You have a lot of music with you? I'd like to hear more of it," Will said. "That piano is sure out of tune. It was Anna's and no one has played it since—"

He stopped and looked at Willie's smiling face. Willie looked down, but when he looked up, he was still smiling at his father.

"Since she died." Will breathed a sigh of relief. For once, Willie hadn't run out of the room at the mention of Anna's death.

"I better go see if I can help Loretta," Grace said.

"No, let the children help. I think we need to talk," said Will. He tweaked Annabelle's cheek and tapped Willie's behind. "Go set the table and see if it doesn't help get you back in Loretta's good graces."

Chapter Eleven

When they were alone, Will walked around the room while Grace stayed at the piano. He didn't say anything for several minutes.

Finally, he cleared his throat and began talking as if she had been privy to his thoughts. "And so, you've come all this way, and I apologize that I didn't know. I hope you understand, if I marry Miss Thompkins, I won't be needing a governess."

"If? I thought you said you were engaged," said Grace.

Will hesitated. "We agreed today to a long engagement. The children need some time to warm up to the idea of having another woman in the house."

"I certainly wouldn't want to be in the way."

Will stared at the beautiful woman sitting patiently on the piano stool. Her hair fell in natural curls as it dried, and something looked familiar about her. Of course! She was wearing that dress he always liked. But she was different from Anna – and from Harriet. He couldn't imagine Grace ever rebuking him for the crime of being on time.

His heart started beating faster in an oddly pleasing way. "You're not in the way," he said. "If you could, do you think you could stay for a while? I can see how much the children love being with you already. It will really help."

"Help them, or ...?" Grace asked.

"Of course, them," Will answered. He had to choose his words carefully. "But also me. Grace, I have to tell you, it's been a hard two years. Annabelle misses her mother, but Willie has never been the same. He feels it was his fault, somehow, when the accident happened."

"I'm so sorry. How did it happen?" she asked softly.

Will related the details of that day. Try as he might, by the end, an edge of anger crept into his voice. "And of course, it wasn't his fault. It was mine. If I had returned to the farm in time, Anna would never have struggled with the cellar door. She'd have been safe inside, and—" he stopped, hardly able to say it.

"And?" Grace said quietly.

"And not gotten swept away." His shoulders slumped.

"From what I've read, no one can withstand the direct force of a tornado. I don't see how it was the fault of either of you."

Will looked up at Grace with tears in his eyes. "But I didn't protect her. I don't understand how this could have happened!"

Grace stood and walked over to Will. She felt the despair flowing out of him, and didn't think he deserved to suffer this kind of guilt.

"She has gone to the Lord. She is resting in peace. She wouldn't want you all to suffer so. I pray that God blesses you with His peace, which he promises *passeth all human understanding.*"

Will dropped his head and his shoulders began to shake. Grace didn't know what to do. He pulled out his handkerchief and blew his nose, but the tears wouldn't stop.

"I'm sorry. I hardly know you, and yet, it feels so good to talk to you," Will said.

Grace took his hand and squeezed it. They stood together as the long rays of the afternoon sun flooded the room with light.

Chapter Twelve

During supper, Will could hardly keep pace with Annabelle's and Grace's conversation as exhaustion set in. Grace offered to see the children up to bed. They left him slowly stirring a spoon in his coffee cup as Grace, Annabelle and Willie mounted the stairs.

Grace helped the twins into their nightclothes and brushed Annabelle's hair. She tucked them under their covers, and sat on Annabelle's bed, hoping to get her to stop talking long enough to fall sleep.

"Annabelle, I know you're tired. If you can hold your questions until morning, I promise I'll answer anything you want to know."

"But I always think of questions at night!" Annabelle said. "All kinds of them! Like, why do some stars twinkle and others don't? How do the spring peeper frogs know its spring and start to peep? And what do you think the Holy Ghost is; is it really a ghost?"

"Let's see," said Grace. "Some stars are farther away than others, so we can't see them twinkling, but they are. And frogs are like other animals; the change of seasons is something they know from instinct. It's how they know when to reproduce, and hibernate for the winter, for example."

"Ohh..." Annabelle said sleepily. She yawned.

Willie lay in his bed, his eyes glued on Grace. He loved how she talked, the way she explained things so he could understand. He was amazed she didn't get mad when she fell in the pond. And – that song she had taught them! The tune and words had been in his head all evening.

"As for the Holy Ghost," said Grace. "That's a deeper subject. But let's just say, that ghost is another word for spirit. And we each have a spirit inside of us, the part of us that never dies. When Jesus left to go to Heaven, he told the disciples not to worry, he would leave his Spirit behind. That way, they could pray and know God was listening."

"I've been praying for someone like you," Annabelle said. "I'm sleepy now. Good night." She turned over and her breathing soon grew steady and deep.

Grace leaned over and gave her a kiss. She went to Willie's bed.

"As for you, don't you have any questions?"

Willie nodded his head, *Yes*.

"Well, are you going to ask me?"

He didn't answer, but he put his fingers out in front of him as if he were playing the piano and his lips mouthed, *Doo-dah*.

"All right, I'll sing very quietly. Remember, you can sing with me if you want." Grace sang the first verse and chorus of *Camptown Races* as if it were a lullaby. After three times through, Willie's eyes finally started to close. She leaned over to give him a kiss, and with her face close to his, she heard him whisper:

"Oh, doo-dah day!"

WILL SAT ON THE FRONT PORCH, smoking a pipe and looking at the stars. Emotional exhaustion gave way to a lightness in his heart. For the first time in years, his mind wasn't replaying the events of two years ago. He should have been embarrassed about breaking down in front of Grace earlier, but instead, he felt only peace.

A soft step fell behind him. Her clear voice spoke up over the night sounds of the farm. "The children are asleep. I'll say good-night, then."

"Would you come out and join me?" asked Will.

She sat down in the rocking chair and pulled her shawl a bit closer. "Annabelle has such an active mind! I just finished explaining about spring peepers and the Holy Spirit."

Will chuckled. "She's been curious since the day she was born. Questions everything! She'll be a handful for some lucky man one day."

"Yes, and a very bright student. Teachers love students who ask questions and seek knowledge. And Will has questions to ask also, when he's ready."

"You know so much about us in such a short time, but I don't know anything about you, Grace Haggerty."

"There's not much to tell, really. My sister and I were raised to value faith and our family more than anything. My father was a bookseller, and we grew up climbing ladders on bookshelves and reading as much as we could. Patty was always better with the customers, and even though I was the eldest, I didn't mind being able to spend more time on my studies. We had to give up the store after father died, though. The money provided for Mother and I after Patty got married..." Her voice trailed off.

"Did you leave your mother behind, then?"

"No, she died two months after our father. At her funeral, neighbors offered sympathy, not for her loss, but for my new status. That's when I first realized they pitied me."

"What status?" Will asked. He stood and walked to the bench next to Grace.

"As an old maid. I had moved past the age of eligibility in their minds. Everyone knew that I had contracted Scarlet fever as a young girl, and probably can't have children. Before

Mother died, I took it as a challenge to find a man who would value me ... for me. But afterwards, even my sister felt I should acquiesce to marrying someone twice my age! I suppose I was in a fit of despair when I submitted my advertisement to paper." Grace's voice caught in her throat. "I thought surely God would help me if I helped myself! Instead, I fear I've just been foolish running off looking for something that I couldn't find at home."

"I don't know," Will said. "I don't think you have a foolish bone in your body."

Grace felt the breeze across her arms and a tingling flowed through her.

"I think I've been trying to force events myself," Will said. "I can't say that I love Harriet. I asked her to marry me for the sake of the children. But now –"

"Now?"

"You are here with me, and it feels as if God sent you to prevent me making the biggest mistake of my life."

Grace didn't know what to say. Her heart swelled with love as she thought of the children asleep upstairs, and Will's loving heart that he seemed to be offering her.

"Will you walk with me?" He smiled down at her, holding out his hand.

She gave it to him and they walked off the porch and out into the night, blending their hearts as they shared their joys and fears with each other.

Chapter Thirteen

*H*arriet Thompson sipped her morning tea as she sat at her desk reading the report. The teacup rattled as she angrily returned it to its saucer.

Lips pursed tightly together, she looked up over her glasses before casting the papers aside.

"How can this be? The nerve!"

"Please don't think I agree," Mr. Busby said nervously. "I'm just the school board secretary. I just take the minutes."

"A school board meeting last night without me in attendance? Why didn't you let me know? I would have told them exactly how I feel about them!"

"It's probably better that you didn't," said Mr. Busby. "The only reason they're considering hiring Professor Sanders as the new headmaster is because they're concerned about the reputation of the school with a woman at the head. An unmarried woman."

"What's that got to do with it?" Harriet fumed. "I've given 100 percent of my time to this school."

"I heard Mr. Jones say, and please understand, it's not me saying this, that the school system's reputation is at risk. He says if a woman won't submit to a husband ruling over her, how can she submit to the authority of the board?"

"Oh, a pox on Mr. Jones. He has hated me since the year I held his son back a grade. Ignoramus."

"He says you can't be reasoned with like a man. He has support on the board," Mr. Busby said. "They're going to interview Professor Sanders, and vote next week!"

One week ... that should be just enough time, Harriet thought. *I can win over the Forrester twins, or at least make Will think I have. It's time to move up the wedding.*

"Mr. Busby," Harriet spoke, her voice noticeably lower and calmer. "I have some business to attend to. Thank you for the very informative discussion. Would you mind relaying to my supporters on the board that I will be making an announcement of marriage very soon?"

"Supporters?" Mr. Busby coughed and spit some of his tea back into his cup. "Yes, yes, your supporters. I'll tell them. But the rest will want to meet him and see if he has the kind of influence with you that gives them the feeling they can appeal to him."

"They have no idea the kind of influence," she said. "Now if you'll please excuse me, I have to be going."

Harriet hurried him out the door. She crossed to her bookshelf, and took out the box which held the trinkets confiscated from disobedient children throughout the school term. She picked out a slingshot for Willie and a small pincushion doll for Annabelle. She'd get the children on her side. *Today.*

"AFTER BREAKFAST, I'll head into town to fetch your trunk. That is, if you're still staying for a couple of weeks," Will said, smiling.

"Yes, I'm staying – for now," she replied. "It will help the children if they learn some addition and subtraction before they start school."

"Yay!" said Annabelle. "I want to learn the piano, too. Mother always said she would teach me."

"Of course," said Grace. "It will take a lot of years of practice, though. But it's not too early to learn the notes and a few songs. Surely Miss Thompkins will see to it you have lessons, once she –"

"Father, will she? I'm not sure she likes me."

Will grew distinctly uncomfortable at the sound of Harriet's name. After his walk with Grace last night, he had woken up thinking only of her. *I've got to re-think this engagement to Harriet. Surely it won't embarrass her if I call it off right away, before she's had a chance to spread the news.*

"Of course she likes you, and Willie, too. Now you both mind Loretta while I'm gone. And no swimming!"

"You can say that again," said Loretta, shaking her head.

Annabelle and Willie raced each other to the parlor and started "playing" the piano.

Loretta put her hands over her ears. "Lord, help me this day!"

"Don't worry." Grace said. "They won't be playing the *Minuet* any time soon, but I'll teach them not to assault our ears in the meantime!"

Will took his leave and Grace began to clear the table.

"Now, Miss Grace, you don't have to do that. I'd rather you put a damper on that noise."

"All right, thank you, Loretta." She smiled and went to the parlor.

"Willie's hogging the stool!" Annabelle complained. "We agreed it's my turn now but he won't get up!"

"Willie, is it Annabelle's turn?"

He shook his head, his fingers continuing to play unrecognizable chords, his mind busy trying to figure out how to make music come out of the keys.

Grace marveled at the natural curve of his fingers. It took her a lot of time to teach most children how to bend them correctly and not slam on the keyboard.

"Annabelle, can you wait a few minutes more? You can learn everything Willie does by watching him, and then it will be your turn to practice. Let's get some chairs from the dining room."

They spent the morning learning how to find Middle C and the other seven whole notes, and to play a scale. Annabelle had her turn, but soon grew bored when music didn't instantly flow from her fingers.

"Can you play for us?" she asked. "I can't make anything pretty come out."

Grace smiled. "I have a song I want to teach you to sing before school. It's the new National Hymn. Would you like to hear it?"

Grace began playing *My Country 'Tis of Thee*, as much as she could from memory. "Oh dear, I just don't know it by heart yet. When your father returns with my trunk, I'll have all my music."

"Do you mind if we stop now? I want to play outside. Come on, Willie!"

The twins raced to the door, threw it open, and nearly ran down Harriet Thompkins.

"Is this the way you greet a visitor?" she said. "I've come to speak with your father. I'll show myself in while you go and find him."

"But he's not home," Annabelle said. "You can wait for him, he won't be long."

"Yes, very good, I'll do just that," said Harriet, and she bustled into the foyer. Music came from the parlor, and she was surprised to see a young woman seated at the piano, eyes closed, playing for no one.

"Ahem." Harriet coughed.

Grace's eyes flew open and her hands lifted off the keyboard. "Oh! You startled me." She stood up.

"Annabelle directed me here to wait for Will. I don't believe we've met. I'm Harriet Thompkins. Are you ... one of the children's cousins?

"Miss Thompkins! I'm ... pleased to meet you." Grace's mind raced, trying to reconcile the cold woman who stood before her with the concept that she could possibly be Will's fiancée. "No, I'm not a cousin. My name is Grace Haggerty, and I'm a ... I'm a friend of the family."

Harriet came in and propped herself on the sofa. She lay down her bag containing the toys on the floor at her feet. She looked at

Grace down her raised nose through her glasses. "I see. I'm pleased to meet you as well. I'd like to meet all of Will's friends as soon as possible, since we will presently be married."

Presently? But Will had said it was to be a long engagement. Grace panicked for a moment at the thought. *Why should it bother me whether he marries her sooner, or later? It's all the same: they are engaged.*

"Have you known the family long?" said Harriet, determined to get more information out of Grace.

"Not long, no. I wouldn't say that," Grace said. Her hands were sweating in her lap. She wanted to flee the room, but her feet wouldn't move.

"No doubt you knew Anna. Poor dear. She was such a sweet woman." Harriet shook her head, more in disapproval than sorrow. "You know, our parents always thought Will and I would marry, ever since we were children."

"I didn't know that," Grace said.

"Yes. That woman bewitched him somehow while I was away getting my education. But it's all for the best. I am now headmistress of the school, and Will and I will finally be together."

"Yes, it's for the best," Grace said. *How could Anna's dying be for anyone's best— except Harriet's?*

An awkward silence descended on the room as the two women looked at each other, Grace with curiosity and Harriet with barely concealed disdain. `

"Miss Grace," Loretta called, bustling into the room. "I've washed your dress and hung it out to dry. I'll help you unpack once Mr. Forrester returns with your –" Loretta stopped in her tracks when she noticed Harriet.

"Unpack? Are you staying here?" Harriet interrupted.

"Just for a short time. Actually, I wasn't planning to stay..." Grace began.

"But you just happened to bring enough clothes to unpack?" Harriet's voice rose in accusation. "This is quite irregular."

Loretta bristled at Harriet's tone. "Mr. Forrester may have house guests if he chooses to, in my opinion."

"I do not believe I was addressing you," Harriet sniffed.

"Hhmph." Loretta knew her place well enough not to get into a direct confrontation, but she didn't have to like backing off. "I'll take my leave. You call me if you need anything, Miss Grace."

"Thank you, Loretta," Grace said. She had to find a way to diffuse the situation and redirect Harriet's attention before she started asking too many questions. "Miss Thompkins, I understand you're a very dedicated teacher."

That was a good enough opening for Harriet to spend the next few minutes extolling her own virtue, and excoriating those who disagreed with her educational theories.

"And to think that the school board is considering hiring a man to replace me. Oh, but I've said too much. Let's talk about you. Where did you say you were from?"

Grace couldn't begin answering questions that she knew Harriet would not like the answers to. She ignored it, and asked about Willie's condition.

"I understand the doctor thinks Willie will talk again one day, when he's ready," she said. "Do you know of any therapies or treatments that would help speed up the process?"

"On the one hand, it's entirely possible that Willie's affliction is nothing that a more vigorous regimen and a good dose of discipline wouldn't fix," Harriet said. "I've told

Will to stop coddling the boy. However, if that doesn't work, I do know of treatments he can receive. In fact, I have a highly regarded friend in Ames who has offered to examine the boy, and admit him if necessary for medicinal treatment."

"Medicinal treatment?" Grace felt panicky at the thought. Willie, in a sanatorium of some kind? She was convinced being separated from Will and Annabelle would set him back further. "I'm more a believer that he is slowly healing on his own, and may quickly improve once he is able to understand the shock he had," Grace said.

"I tell you, an examination is required to know for sure. What if he doesn't come out of this on his own? He'll be crippled for life. What sort of work can a mute boy ever hope to have? No, the situation for him must be diagnosed and remedied, and the sooner the better," said Harriet.

Grace traced one finger over the piano keys. Maybe Harriet was right. It had already been two years since Anna died, two years since Willie had spoken. She felt she understood him and could communicate with him, but how would he be able to learn in school without speaking and having normal friendships with the other children?

The two women jumped when they heard a loud clattering sound on the porch, and the front door burst open. Willie and Anna appeared, hunched over one end of Grace's trunk.

"Keep going! Just set it down at the bottom of the stairs!" Will said to them. He came through the door behind him holding up the other end of the trunk.

The three of them set the trunk down on the floor. "Whew, that was heavy!" Annabelle said.

Harriet and Grace stood up at the same time. "There you are!" Harriet called from the parlor.

Will's eyes registered shock as he looked from Harriet's face to Grace's and back. "Harriet! I had no idea you were coming. How are you?" He crossed the room toward her and held out his hand.

She took it and pulled him in closer, raising her cheek.

"I just couldn't wait another day to see you and these darling children!" Harriet said.

"Hello, Miss Thompkins," said Annabelle. Willie came in and stood next to the piano.

"Annabelle, come sit by me," said Harriet, patting the sofa next to her. Annabelle crossed the room and sat. "I've something for you today; would you like to see?"

Harriet reached in to her bag and pulled out the cloth doll. "Here, this is for you."

"Thank you! Look, Father!" Annabelle said.

"And you, young man. You can come closer," Harriet said.

Willie didn't move.

"Wouldn't you like to see what I have for you?" she beckoned.

Willie half shrugged one shoulder. But when Harriet pulled out the slingshot, he moved close enough to take it out of her hand. He fingered the wood and leather, grinned shyly, and nodded his head to Harriet in thanks.

"What do you say?" she asked. "Surely you remember your manners!"

Willie nodded his head a little more emphatically and bowed a bit to show his thanks.

"Hmmm. We'll have to work on this," Harriet said.

Will broke in. "This is very thoughtful of you," he said. He looked at Grace with a questioning eye.

Grace felt like an actress who was about to be booed off the stage and pelted with tomatoes. Everything about the scene before her was wrong, and fake, and she was pretending to go along with it. She couldn't be a part of it for one more minute.

She stood abruptly. "Please excuse me. I've not been feeling well this morning. If you don't mind, I'll just be resting upstairs."

Will moved to take her elbow and escort her from the room. "I'm sorry to hear that," he said. "Can Loretta bring you up something? Do you need anything in your trunk? I can bring it up to you."

"That won't be necessary," she said. "I'll be fine if I can just lie down for a few minutes."

Grace walked out of the room, forcing herself not to run at full pace up the stairs. She couldn't be a part of this family with Harriet in the picture. Will had made his choice, and whatever part she could play was over. She couldn't pretend to be a friend or the children's governess or even piano teacher. She knew in her heart, she would have to leave.

Chapter Fourteen

his is wrong, this is so wrong, Will thought. The long dinner would never be over, he was sure of it. The sound of Harriet's voice had become like a piece of straw scratching him somewhere in his shirt and he jumped at the chance to take the tray Loretta had made for Grace up to her room.

Will knocked gently on Grace's door, careful not to upend the toast and cup of tea in the other hand.

"Grace? We've had dinner and I didn't want to disturb you."

No reply.

He gently rapped again.

Silence.

"I've brought you a cup of tea."

"Come in."

Will opened the door and was surprised to see Grace sitting up in a chair. Her reticule was packed and sitting on the bed.

"Are you feeling better?"

"I'm fine."

Will set the tray down on the dressing table. He didn't like the look in her eyes or the tone of her voice. He felt so distant from her, yet they were there together in her small room.

"I'll be taking Harriet back to town now," Will said.

Grace acknowledged the statement with a blink of her eyes.

"I had no idea she was coming today," Will explained. "In fact, I stopped by her house earlier but she wasn't there. I wanted to speak with her alone, before things went too far. Grace, I'm going to break off the engagement to her. I have to."

Grace raised an eyebrow. "I don't think that would be wise," she said.

"You don't? But ... you do have feelings for me, don't you? I want more time to get to know you. No, that's not even the truth. I don't need more time – I know what my heart is telling me. Grace, I love you and want you to stay. I need you. The children need you. Grace, will you marry me?"

"Will Forrester, you cannot be engaged to two people at the same time! Harriet obviously has feelings for you and the children. She can help them in ways I cannot. She said you two were promised to each other as children, is that true?"

Will nodded his head, not believing what she was saying. He had been so certain that his feelings for her were true. Surely she had the same feelings for him. He had felt them and seen it in her eyes. He had heard nothing but love in the sound of her voice. He had seen the children embrace her and welcome them into their home and lives.

"I know, I should not have asked you before speaking with Harriet. But I am leaving now and I will end my engagement with her. When I return, can we pick up where we left off last night? I mean, I want you to stay, and when the time is right, our hearts will know what to do."

He searched her face for any sign that she might have heard his words, but more than that, felt their meaning in her heart. He knew one thing only: He wanted her to stay more than anything in his life.

"I'm afraid that won't be possible," Grace said. "I've decided to write to another gentleman who responded to my advertisement. I think this has been a mistake from the start."

Mistake? Mistake! The word echoed in Will's mind like a gunshot. It was a lie. She was lying. There was nothing about her arrival in Fair Isle that had been a mistake.

"I don't understand," he said quietly. "Grace, please stay."

GRACE'S MIND RACED through her possible answers. Her heart screamed at her to say yes, to just stay and wait to see what would happen. But she had seen Harriet's determination. She wouldn't let Will off the hook that easily. The children would have to attend her school, and she would make their lives miserable if the engagement were broken.

Besides, she could get Willie the help he needed.

Grace had to do something to stop herself from rushing into his arms. The sadness in his voice and his tacit accusation that she wasn't telling him the truth hit her with a force that she had never felt before. She wanted to tell him that she loved him, and Annabelle, and Willie most of all.

"William?" Harriet's voice rose up the stairs. "We must be going! I have to finish my work for the day. Are you coming?"

The grating sound pierced the moment, and Grace stood. "Thank you for the tea."

"I'll be back, and we'll talk," Will said.

When the door was closed, Grace flung herself on the bed. Hot tears rolled down her face as the image of his pained face filled her mind. At the same time, she was embarrassed for ever coming here and putting herself in the middle of this situation. Obviously, Will had already planned for his own happiness and the well-being of the children by asking Harriet to marry him. It would all work out for them. Willie would get the help he needed, and the children would get the best education at Harriet's school. Loretta would shower them with love, and they would make it.

Grace calmed down a bit. She had to get moving. She dried her tears and stood up. There was only one thing to do. She would leave before Will returned. She couldn't bear to tell him no again.

Chapter Fifteen

race took one look around the room, picked up her reticule and went to say good-bye to the children. She would go the same way she came; walk back to town, and book passage on the first train. She could send for her trunk from wherever she ended up.

Loretta was in the kitchen washing the dishes. Grace looked for the children, and found them outside on the front porch.

Annabelle was in the porch swing and Willie in the rocker. Their faces were sweaty from running back and forth in the yard. It seemed they never stopped racing, challenging each other, but the competition only spurred each of them on. They loved each other more than anyone else.

"We were just going to come see how you were," Annabelle said. "I wish you were at lunch with us. Miss Thompkins talked the whole time."

"I'm a little better now," Grace said. Willie saw the reticule in her hand, and stood up. "I have something to tell you, something very important." She sat down on the porch steps. Annabelle sat on her right and Willie on her left.

"When I first saw you swimming in the pond, Annabelle, I don't think I've ever seen a happier little girl. I want you to always remember to look on the sunny side and find that joy wherever you can in life. Your gift is to bring it to other people." Grace gave her a hug.

"And Willie, when I saw how stubborn you were, not swimming, I thought, 'Now there's a boy who will grow up knowing his own mind.' I'm glad you did swim, and I know you can do whatever you put your mind to."

Willie looked at Grace with a question in his eyes.

"I hope someday, you'll find the words you think are important enough to say out loud. I believe you will. I hope you will use your gifts of careful thinking and fierce empathy to help others overcome their own difficulties. I believe in you."

Grace's voice faltered. "And now, I'm going to say good-bye."

"No!!" Annabelle cried.

Willie jumped up and stood in front of Grace, ready to block her way.

"I don't want to, really, but this has all been a mistake. I'll always be grateful you answered my advertisement. I believe your prayers for a mother will be answered in a different way."

"Miss Thompkins? She's nothing like a mother," Annabelle said.

Willie crossed his arms in front of him.

"She's not like your mother was, no. But you're getting to an age where having a smart woman like Miss Thompkins in your corner will be a big advantage. You'll understand one day. And meantime, Loretta loves you like her own children. And your father – " Grace swallowed hard. "Your father loves you fiercely. That will never change."

Grace kissed Annabelle's hair and stood up. She tried to put her arms around Willie. He stood still as a statue.

"I'll write to you, and we'll always be friends," Grace said.

Willie turned and ran away to the barn.

"Where will you go?" asked Annabelle.

"Right now, I'm not sure. But I'm not going back to New Jersey. I'll find my place in this world, and let you know as soon as I'm settled."

Annabelle nodded, tears rolling down her cheeks.

"Would you do me a favor and tell Loretta good-bye for me?"

"What about Father?"

"I've already told him. Take care, sweet Annabelle." Grace picked up her reticule and started walking toward the lane.

Annabelle couldn't believe she was leaving. She ran into the house to find Loretta, hoping for a chance Grace could be convinced to stay.

"AND SO, HARRIET, I'm sorry to have misled you."

"Misled me? That's what you did before you married Anna. But now? This is breaking your word!"

"I'm sorry. Again. It's all I can tell you. You can't possibly think we would truly be happy together? The children would vex you to no end."

"I admit it would have taken an adjustment on my part. And extra effort at the end of my long days to properly train them," Harriet said. "But I swear to you, Will Forrester, while I will not hinder them in school, nor will I go out of my way to help them. Surely you could consider their well-being."

Is she threatening my children? Any good feelings Will had for Harriet vanished in the moment. He looked at her puckered up face, hot with anger, and wondered how he had ever even placed his lips on her cheeks. If she wanted a war, he would fight fire with fire.

"Harriet, I'm a man of few words, usually. I keep to myself. But so help me God, if I get even a whiff of a notion that you're not fully participating in a positive way in my children's education, that anything you might say or do would be detrimental to them, or if you harbor any ill will toward them, I will personally see to it that every man on the school board knows exactly what you are doing – and why."

Harriet stepped back away from him. She sputtered and sneered at him, but obviously thought better of saying anything. She gave a quick nod of her head, turned on her heel, and stalked off into her house.

A bolt of lightning lit the western sky as if to punctuate the breakup. Will looked up just as a crack of thunder rolled across the fields. Other people on the street started hurrying along, and shopkeepers came out to bring in their signs and produce bins.

He watched the large, dark clouds to get an idea of the direction of the storm. They were rolling and billowing to the west of town. Soon, they moved closer and he looked out of town down the road. The storm would soon be overhead and reach the farm.

He jumped into the cart, turned the horse as fast as he could, and headed home to his children – and Grace. Love for her swelled in his heart, and he could not rest until he knew she was his.

Chapter Sixteen

race walked clumsily down the lane, her reticule bumping at her side as she pushed forward against the wind. She hadn't seen the storm clouds when she left the farm, but now the entire sky was dark and ominous. She considered stopping for shelter along the road, but thought if she could just get to town, she could wait in safety at the train station.

The sky lit up with a bright light against the gray clouds. A crack of thunder almost immediately followed. She bent her head forward and put two hands to the handle of her bag, willing herself to run.

"Grace! Grace, stop!" A voice came calling on the wind. Will's horse came rushing to a stop and he was looking down from the cart. "Where are you going? Get in! Quickly!!"

Grace looked up, raindrops starting to fall against her face. "I have to get to the train station!" she yelled.

"Not now, there's no time! We have to get back to the house! There could be a twister in those clouds, and if it gets there before I do ..."

She jumped at the realization and ran to the other side of the cart to climb in. Will grabbed her bag and threw it in the back, then raced off down the lane.

The wind was practically blowing them home. Leaves on the trees were waving inside out, and Grace was too afraid to look behind her. Will drove the horse straight into the barn, and yelled, "Get to the house! Take Loretta and the children to the storm cellar. I'll meet you right there!" He didn't wait for her to answer as he began unhitching the horse and securing him in his stall.

Grace ran to the kitchen door and burst in. "Loretta! Annabelle! Willie!" she called. She ran through the main floor rooms and called up the stairs. *They must have seen this coming. Loretta would have already taken them.*

Grace raced out back to the storm cellar door, reached down and opened it on creaking hinges. Annabelle's cries reached her ears first.

"We have to find him! Let me go, Loretta!" Grace climbed down into the dark.

"Miss Grace! Thank the Lord!" said Loretta. "You have to find Willie!"

Willie. He's in the barn. Surely he'll come with Will.

"Will is in the barn with him, they're coming!" she said. "We have to close the door and wait."

Grace reached outside and grabbed the handle. She shut the door and sat next to Loretta and Annabelle in the dark. She had never been through this kind of storm before, hiding underground, wondering if everything on the surface would be destroyed. *No, not Willie,* she prayed. *Please, Lord. Protect Will and his son.*

They heard the steel door hinges squeak and Will's face appeared. "Grace? Are you in here? Is everyone here?"

"Yes, we're here, but not Willie! I saw him run to the barn earlier. Didn't he come with you?"

"No!" Will was perched on one knee. He looked up at the clouds. "I can see a funnel cloud in the distance, but I have time. Leave the door open for 5 minutes. If I'm not back by then, close it and bar it!"

"What? Wait! Don't –" Grace called, but his face had disappeared.

Will was unstoppable. He ran back to the barn he had just secured, threw open the door and called up into the hayloft. "Willie! I know you're up there! Please, come with me now! Willie!"

He couldn't hear anything over the howling of the wind. He started to climb the ladder, when a few pieces of hay fell on him. He looked up to see Willie, crying, looking down at him.

Will's heart leaped. *Thank you, God!* He reached out his hand. "Come down, son! We have to get to the shelter!"

Willie shook his head. *No.*

"There's no time! Come down this instant! You'll be safe with me. I promise! With Annabelle, Loretta ... and Grace."

110

Willie disappeared for a moment and Will started climbing after him. Before he could reach the top, Willie's foot appeared on the top rung. The little boy clutched his treasure box under one arm and started climbing down the ladder.

Will scrambled down and leaped to the floor. "Jump!" He called. Willie jumped into his arms. Will raced back outside the barn and put Willie down. The wind was blowing shingles off the roof of the house, and the porch swing was banging into the wall. The trees were bending over at the edge of the fields, and a large tornado was flinging dirt high into the air.

Will bolted the barn door, grabbed his son, and ran for the shelter. Grace emerged, reaching for the door to close it, when Will nearly knocked her inside.

"Get in! Get in!" he yelled. He tossed Willie down the stairs, grabbed the metal door behind him, and slammed it shut as the storm screamed and howled overhead.

Loretta had lit a small lamp and was sitting with Annabelle in her lap along the back wall between a crate half-full of potatoes and a bag of onions. Grace was checking

Willie all over, hugging him and crying. Willie clung to her waist.

Will's chest was heaving and he could hardly catch his breath in the damp, closed space. He wrapped his arms around Grace and Willie and felt his heart begin to slow down a bit.

Grace turned to him and started to cry with fear. "Oh Will! I thought I'd lost you – both of you!"

Will hugged her in close. "I've got you. I've got you," he whispered, over and over.

Chapter Seventeen

The storm raged overhead as the family huddled in the shelter. They could hear pieces of wood and rocks hitting the cellar door, and then the sound of hail pounding down.

"It's a bad one, all right," Will said. "I pray the animals make it through."

Grace didn't know what to say. She saw Will's eyebrows furrowed deeply over his eyes, and he rested his head in his hands. Annabelle and Willie seemed to be far off, as if in a nightmare of their own. She couldn't imagine the images of the last storm that were playing through their minds.

She started to speak the words of a hymn, and then the tune came to her and her voice got stronger as she began to sing:

Our God, our Help in ages past,

Our Hope for years to come,

Our Shelter from the stormy blast,

And our eternal Home!

"I love that one," Loretta said. She joined her voice with Grace's for the second verse:

Under the shadow of Thy throne

Thy saints have dwelt secure;

Sufficient is Thine arm alone,

And our defense is sure.

Their voices rose together, and soon the family was singing every hymn and song they could remember. Willie was silent but his face looked more peaceful.

Suddenly, the wind stopped outside and Grace looked with happiness at Will. "It's over!"

"Not quite," Will said. "I reckon we're about halfway through. The eye of the storm is passing. We'll have more of it on the other side."

Even Grace's hope began to fade. Willie saw her dejection, and tugged at her sleeve.

Doo-dah. He mouthed.

Grace smiled. She was exhausted with fear and her heart just wasn't in such a song at a time like this. She shook her head at him, *No*.

Willie's smile turned into concern. She had taught him about music and love and acceptance. And Father had come to find him, and they were all safe. He was worried about the animals, but everything he loved was right here in the cellar.

"C-c-c-amp town ladies s-s-ing this song..." he whispered.

In the dead quiet, his voice cracked and squeaked.

"Camptown racetrack's five miles long –" he said in a louder tone. Willie stopped and licked his lips. Then as loud as his poor voice could muster, he sang, "Oh, doo-dah day!"

Will stood up so fast, he bumped his head on the low ceiling. "Willie!"

Annabelle hugged him and jumped up and down.

Grace and Willie kept their eyes on each other's faces. His broke into a wide smile. She nodded, and they continued together at the top of their lungs:

> *Goin' to run all night! Goin' to run all day!*
>
> *I bet my money on a bob-tailed nag,*
>
> *Somebody bet on the bay!*

Loretta looked at their faces shining in the lamplight as Grace, Willie, Annabelle and Will sang the verses, as loud as they could, even louder than the wind that had started up overhead. Once they started, they couldn't stop, and sang the song all the way through over and over.

Praise God! She smiled and clapped along with them until the wind blew itself out and they all emerged together into the light of a new day.

Epilogue

Three months later...

"Welcome home, Mrs. Forrester!"

"Why, thank you, kind sir!" Grace took Will's hand and stepped into the new front entrance of their home. The storm had torn off half the roof, and it had taken months to repair it and replace the water-damaged floors and broken windows.

The family had been living in town while the work was completed. Annabelle and Willie had started school, and Grace was assured by Harriet that they would be in the same class together.

"It's beautiful," she said. "You have worked so hard to get this done before the weather turns."

"What choice did I have, my love? I feared you'd run off for real this time if you had to stay in three rooms with two very loud children much longer." Will laughed.

"Ha ha, very funny," she said, smacking him on the arm. "And who would have helped you answer both Annabelle's and Willie's questions then, hmm?"

"You have a point, my dear," he said. "I'm not sure there are enough hours in the day to answer Willie's questions. He's got two years of backlog to work off."

They walked into the parlor, holding hands. Grace ran her fingers over the piano keys. It was even more badly out of tune than before.

"I'll see if I can wrangle someone to come out here and look at that as soon as I can," Will said. "Feel I owe it to you."

"It's all right. There will be plenty of time for singing." She pondered whether to tell Will the news. She could hardly believe it herself, but the doctor had been certain.

"Before the children get here, there is something I want to tell you," Will said. "I love you. I've loved you since the minute I saw you. Actually, it was the second minute, when you came up out of the pond!"

"Who would believe a girl only had to dunk herself to get a man's attention?" Grace said, laughing. "And I love you, Will. Ever since I saw you understand Willie without any words. I knew your heart was bigger than any man's I've ever known."

They kissed and looked into each other's eyes.

"I'm the happiest man who ever lived!" Will said. "I don't want a single thing more than you, Annabelle and Willie."

"Ahem, I do hope you want just one more thing," Grace said.

"What could that be?"

"Another child?" she asked.

"I'm perfectly content."

"What if you don't have any choice in the matter?"

Will held her at arm's length and cocked his head to one side. "Are you ...? But I thought you ... Are you sure? Grace, really?"

She smiled and nodded her head. "I'm going to have a baby, Will!"

"Yahoo!" Will pumped his fist into the air and jumped around as if he were Annabelle and Willie rolled into one. He grabbed Grace by the waist and spun her around.

She laughed and threw her arms around his neck, put her feet down and leaned on him, drawing strength and love from his strong arms, feeling its warmth and the happiness of the new life growing deep within her.

About the Author

*L*orena Dove has been reading and dreaming about living during the great westward migration since she was a young child growing up in New York and then Virginia. A descendent of Italian and German immigrants, she enjoys the interplay of cultures and passing down of traditions, recipes and family values to her children and grandchildren.

Lorena raised four children in a modernized 1880s log cabin for 10 years in West Virginia. The seasons of nature, the beauty of the mountains and rivers, and the simple enjoyment of gardening, reading and quilting have been her passions.

She lives with her husband, a retired Marine Corps colonel, and sons in Virginia. She collaborates on books with her daughter, whose passion for historical fiction exceeds her own, and is waiting for her granddaughters to fit into their mother's dress-up hoopskirts and bonnets.

You can keep in touch with Lorena by visiting her on Facebook at LorenaDoveBooks, or sign up for her VIP Readers Group at LorenaDove.com.

THE SWEET LAND OF LIBERTY BRIDES SERIES

Book 1: Giovanna: *The Cowboy's Calabrese Mail Order Bride* ~ Can a young Italian widow win the love of a Nordic cowboy in time to save the only thing she loves?

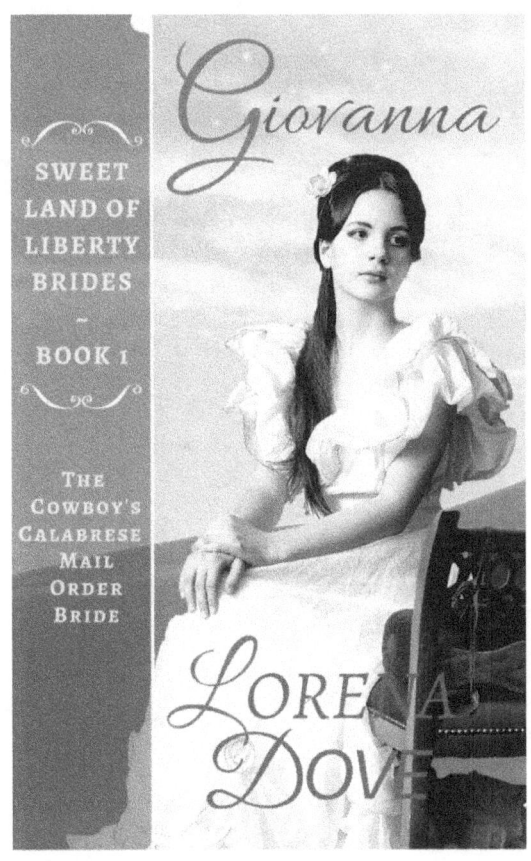

Book 2: **Nathalie**: *The Circuit Rider's Rhineland Mail Order Bride* ~ Can practical Nathalie find love in the strong arms of an intellectual dreamer?

Book 3: *Silvia*: *The Stockman's Slovak Mail Order Bride* ~ Silvia flees a violent past and heads to the west hoping for safety and dreaming of love. Can Dell, a 'Black Irish' stockman and reformed fighter, win her heart if he must fight for it?

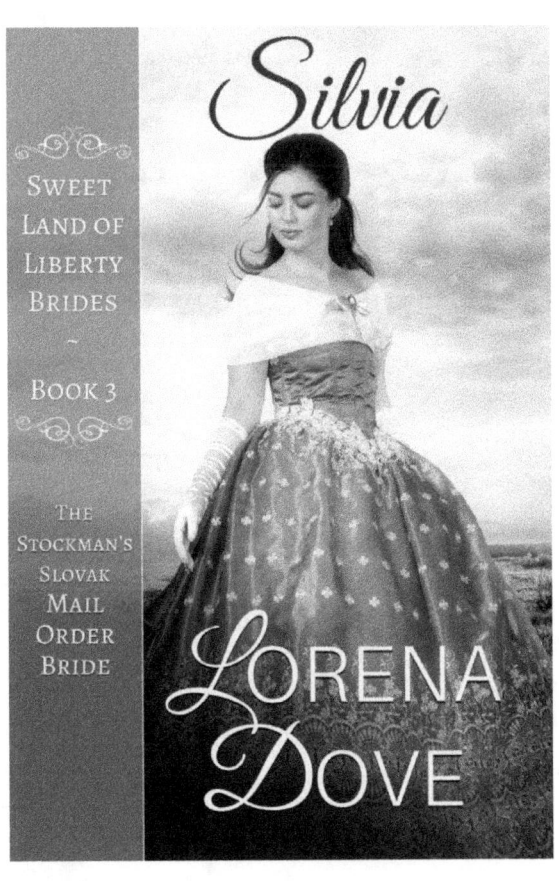

Book 4: *Louisa*: *Cap Garland's Irish Mail Order Bride ~*
` Read below for a free sample of **Louisa.**

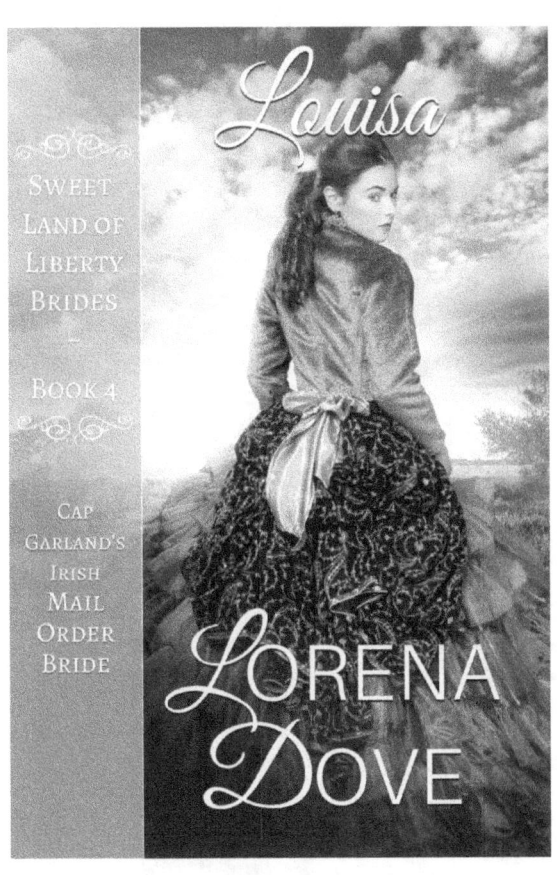

Giovanna:

The Cowboy's Calabrese Mail Order Bride

"What is your name, child?" The large, imposing woman towered over the small creature crouching at the edge of the street. "Goodness gracious, a person could break her ankle stumbling over you!" Mrs. Forsythe waved her handkerchief at her face and peered over her thick glasses.

The small girl froze in place, her hand stretched out toward a dirty biscuit she was trying to scoop up off the sooty, mud-covered street.

"R-R-Rosa," she stammered, looking up with tears in her large brown eyes.

The giant of a woman stood over Rosa, her thin lips set in a grim line, the flowers on her elaborate hat twitching disapproval in time to her shaking head. Rosa cowered beneath her, drawing herself into an even smaller bundle of calico and long black hair. The woman's shadow grew over Rosa as she leaned down. Rosa trembled and closed her eyes tightly shut.

"Rosa. Well then. Ahem," said the woman. "Let me help you with those. Where's your mother?"

Rosa opened her eyes to see the thin lips curled into a genuine smile as Mrs. Forsythe reached across her to retrieve one of the errant biscuits. She burst into tears of relief and self-reproach.

"M-m-mama's inside the church, and I've dropped her basket!"

"Did she buy you all these biscuits?" asked Mrs. Forsythe with one eyebrow raised.

"No, Ma'am! Mama sells biscuits and today I'm helping. Or I'm supposed to be ..." her words trailed off as she fumbled with the ruined goods. "She works hard to bake enough and now these are ruined," Rosa paused to wipe off her tears. "She'll be sad."

Mrs. Susan Forsythe was hardly accustomed to scrambling around in the dirt at the edge of the street. Her normal Sunday practice was to go directly home after church to rest up from her busy week at the milliner's shop, paying no attention to the street vendors who didn't have the money for a permanent stand in the market, much less a spacious storefront like hers.

Whatsoever ye do for the least of these, ye do for Me. The pastor's sermon text echoed in her mind as she considered the dark-haired waif.

"Hand me the basket while you pick up the rest of them," she directed.

"Rosa? Rosa! Where are you?" The rising voice came to their ears across the church courtyard as a petite woman dressed in black rushed about looking this way and that for her daughter.

"Over here!" Mrs. Forsythe waved and pointed down at Rosa.

"What's happened?" Giovanna said in her heavy Italian accent. "Are you hurt, Rosa? The biscuits are covered in soot! *Che sfortuna!* What bad luck!" Giovanna's natural temper and talk-ativeness were winding up into a tirade.

"I'm sorry, Mama. I stood by the steps liked you asked, but I saw a kitty and thought if I could catch it and bring it home, Pearl would have a friend. I didn't mean to trip and drop the basket, Mama! I'm so very sorry." The tip of Rosa's nose was the only part of her face not streaked with soot or tears as she stood twisting her small hands in her dress.

Giovanna's heart went out to her daughter, so delicate and frail but always concerned about her kitten and any other animal she saw.

"Don't you worry now, Rosa, I can bake some more, and these we can feed to Pearl." Giovanna wiped away Rosa's tears with the apron of her skirt and kissed her tenderly on her forehead.

Rosa buried her face in her mother's black shirtfront, then smiled and looked up at the woman who had helped her.

"Hello! I'm Susan Forsythe," the woman said briskly with her hand outstretched. "When I wasn't tripping over her, I was just helping your daughter with the fallen biscuits."

"Giovanna Ransoni." Taking Mrs. Forsythe's hand, Giovanna tried to make light of her losses even though she hadn't the money for more flour with a day's wages lost in the dirt. "I made these biscuits to sell, but I'm afraid they'll have to be eaten by the animals now."

"Could I buy half your basket right now, if you're selling?"

"God bless you, Ma'am!" Giovanna said, astonished at the generous offer coming from this stern, stout woman. "But they're all broken and dirty."

"Never you mind! I can brush them off and use them for a pudding. Mr. Forsythe will never know," she said with a wink. "On second thought, give me all you have."

Mrs. Forsythe pressed some money into Giovanna's hand and scooped up the biscuits into her shawl, tying them into a tidy pouch. "I don't like to see food go to waste and these look delicious—at least, they did!" With a quick turn to step into her waiting carriage, she called out, "Take care, little Rosa! Good-bye, Giovanna!"

The driver loosened the brake and chucked the reins on the horse's back. As the carriage lurched away from the curb and down the street, Giovanna said, "Rosa, what do the letters say?" She pointed to the sign on the door of the retreating buggy.

"F-O-R—For—S-Y—Forsythe   MILL-IN-ER-Y. Forsythe Millinery, Mama." Rosa looked up at her mama and smiled after she puzzled it out.

"*Brava!* Such a smart girl, my Rosa. One day, you'll teach me to read in English, too," Giovanna said. She looked down at the crumple of bills in her hand, pushed them into the pocket under her apron, and hurried home to count them in private.

Pick up your copy of **Giovanna** today to read her full story and begin the Sweet Land of Liberty Brides series set in late 1800s South Dakota.

ALSO BY LRENA DOVE

Mail Order Bride: Saved by Grace,~ Fraternal twins, Annabelle and Willie, whose widowed father is about to remarry, send for a mail-order bride to prevent him marrying a woman they hate. Can Grace Haggerty overcome her embarrassment that Will does not want her for a wife?

Mail Order Bride: Celia's Secret Baby, Book 7 in the Blessed with Babies multi-author series from the Clean & Wholesome Book Club ~ Abandoned as a child, Celia determines to carry on with her plan to be a mail order bride even after the death of her best friend at the orphanage. Thomas is still under the thumb of a sister who is trying to run his life. Can Thomas forgive Celia for keeping something so secret as a baby—one she had given his name?

Mail Order Bride: Angie's Hope, Book 7 in the
Valentine's Day Mail Order Brides series from the
Clean & Wholesome Book Club ~ Angie is ready for
her engagement to expire when she meets and falls in
love with Cal. But her brother in Kansas City now has
different plans for her that don't include Cal. Can
Angie marry the man who truly loves her before it's
too late?

Christmas Bride: Susan's Secret Baby ~ A widow with a secret heads to the Oklahoma Territories as a possible wife for a lonely farmer with three children.

Find these and all new releases by Lorena Dove on Amazon, or visit

http://www.LorenaDove.com

http://www.Facebook.com/LorenaDoveBooks